ALSO BY JAMES NOLL

Tales of the Weird
A Knife in the Back
You Will Be Safe Here
Burn All The Bodies
Mad Tales (Compendium)
Don't Turn Around (Illustrated Compendium)
Thirteen Tales (Short Story Compilation)

The Bonesaw Trilogy
The Rabbit, The Jaguar, & The Snake

The Topher Trilogy (Novels):
Raleigh's Prep
Tracker's Travail
Topher's Ton
The Topher Trilogy (Omnibus)

Serials
The Hive: Season 1

Non-Fiction
Being Indie: Tips, Tricks, and Tactics for the Beginning Indie Author

Audio Books
A Knife in the Back
Thirteen Tales
The Hive: Season 1 (Coming Soon!)

Jason King & The Konami Code

James Noll

PULP!
Horror, Post-Apocalyptic, and Science Fiction

This is a work of fiction. Names, characters, places, and incidents either are products of the author's imagination or are used fictitiously and are not to be construed as real. Any resemblance to actual events, locales, organizations, or persons, living or dead, is entirely coincidental. I tell you true

JASON KING & THE KONAMI CODE.
Copyright © 2018 by James Noll
All rights reserved. Printed in the United States of America. No part of this book may be used or reproduced in any manner without written permission except in the case of brief quotations embodied in critical articles and reviews. For information, visit www.jamesnoll.net

PULP books may be purchased for educational, business, or sales promotional use. For information, visit www.jamesnoll.net

Book design by James Noll

Cover by Grant Ervin

Cover design by Grant Ervin

Author Photo by Haley Noll

ISBN: 1985860589
ISBN-13: 978-1985860582 (Createspace)

This one's for my fans, all of those intrepid souls who took a risk on a guy at a table at a convention or a festival. Thank you!

CONTENTS

Jason King & The Konami Code   1
Best Dog I Ever Had (Sneak Peak of *The Hive!*) 33

Jason King & The Konami Code

Jason was playing *Castlevania* in his hiding place when a PM popped up and blocked the screen. It was Gary.
Baseball. Alley. Twenty.
Ugh.
Gary was his best friend. Usually, they just hung out and played video games together. Classic NES 8-bits were their favorite. *Contra, Zelda, Metroid, Super Mario Bros.* They were, of course, obsessed with *Castlevania*, especially after Jason discovered the Konami Code. Two seconds of up up, down down, left right, left right, B A Start and they got thirty lives each. More than enough to win. But after they conquered the game that way a few times, he and Gary got bored. It wasn't fun when you cheated. So they stopped. If they were going to play it, they were going to do it right, with stakes, when every decision mattered.

If Jason was obsessed with computers and coding, Gary was obsessed with baseball. America's pastime. He inherited it from his father who, before the Tlek invasion, played for a minor league team that developed its players for the City Sentinels. Every second he wasn't holed up with Jason playing NES, he was outside throwing an old baseball around, the one signed by all the Sentinels the last time they won the World Series. And if he wasn't doing that, he was looking for a game or setting one up.

Jason didn't mind playing baseball. In fact, he kind of enjoyed it. But right then when Gary contacted him, he was right in the middle of a great *Castlevania* run. He'd gotten the firearm and made it to Level 6. No way he was going to stop now. Then his mother called to him from the kitchen.

"Jason? Have you cleaned out your closet like I told you to?"

"Not yet!"

"Seriously, Jason. There are wires spilling out everywhere."

Jason groaned again. He deleted what he'd already written ("level six can't make it"), replacing it with "OMW!"

Jason's hiding place was kind of like a dumbwaiter, only quadruple the size. His mom told him that when the building had first been constructed people used it for moving or, when the building offered laundry service, to transport their dirty clothes to and from the basement. It had been out of commission for a long time, but Jason had hacked into the electricity make it run. Then he set up an app he could use to operate it from his computer. Other than Gary and his mother, nobody else knew about it. He didn't have to worry about the building supervisor finding out. He was too busy tending to the never-ending stream of appliance breakdowns. Before his mother could say anything else, he opened up the app and clicked on the "down" button.

Gary was out in the alley, tossing his ball against a mini-trampoline they'd found in the sewers a few weeks back. One leg was broken and there was a rip in the top, which made using it unpredictable. That was the point.

"About time," Gary said, jumping to field a crazy bounce. "Aren't you tired of that stupid game yet?"

Jason adjusted his backpack, comfortable with the familiar weight of his laptop. He took it with him wherever he went.

"I was on Level Six."

"Konami?"

"Nope."

That made Gary pause.

"Whoa."

He threw the ball one more time, scooping it up off the concrete.

"Let's go. There's a game at the old mill parking lot."

They cut through the familiar alleys of the city, keeping track of the Silver Bullet the entire time. The Silver Bullet was the skyscraper that the Single Corp owned. It was their home base, and it employed nearly half the city, including Jason's mom. They used it as a kind of north star, a beacon they could always rely on to maintain their bearings.

It took them twenty minutes to make it to the other side of town, where they stopped at the tunnel that led to the Industrial District. There were several tunnels like it all over the city, some even closer to Jason's building, but most of them had been flooded. This one was closest to the Silver Bullet, and the Single Corp made sure to keep it clear and clean. It was also the territory of the Black Shirts—older bullies who liked to harass Jason and all his friends. The boys stood outside the entrance, trying to decide whether or not to go inside. Finally, Gary said, "I don't want to go."

"Stop being a baby," Jason said. He grabbed his friend's arm and pulled. "You're the one who wanted to play baseball."

Gary shook the entire way through, and Jason walked the line between being irritated by his friend and commiserating with him. The tunnel was dark. It smelled like mold and cigarettes. Gangs had graffitied it with their signs: the calligraphy of the CBCKs, the devil's horns of the 9th Street Sinners, the swollen face of the Puglies. Even worse was the sign of the Black Shirts: a snake strangling the sun. Jason kept waiting for something to loom up at them from some dark shadow, and both of them took a nice, deep breath when they emerged on the other side.

"See," Jason said. "Nothing to —"

"Well, well, well," somebody said.

The boys froze. The voice had come from behind them.

"Look what we got here, D'mitri. A couple of stupid kids."

Jason and Gary glanced at each other. Should they make a break for it?

"Don't even think about running, you little jerks," a second voice said. D'mitri. "You make me chase you and you'll be sorry. Turn around."

Gary did, followed by Jason.

Two Black Shirts were sitting in the weed-covered hill on either side of the tunnel opening, their motorcycles parked off to the side. One hopped down and strutted up to them. He was short but fit, with veiny, wiry muscles. One side of his head was completely shaved. On it was a tattoo of a snake strangling the sun.

"What you hiding behind your back?" he said, pointing at Gary.

"Nothing."

"Nothing, huh? Give it here."

Gary started to as he was told, but Jason stopped him.

"Don't. That's yours."

The older boy poked him in the shoulder, pushing him back.

"Shut up," he said. Then to Gary, "Give it here."

Gary paused and D'mitri slapped him across the face.

"Now!"

Jason balled up his fists, but Gary said, "It's okay."

He took his baseball out from behind his back, his prized baseball, and handed it over. D'mitri smirked.

"That's a good boy. Now you. Tough guy. Your backpack."

Jason glowered.

"I'm not afraid of you," he said.

D'mitri smiled.

"Oh yeah? You should be."

He reached out and grabbed his arm, but Jason ripped it away. D'mitri's face hardened.

"Come on D," his friend yelled, laughing. "You gonna let a little kid do that to you?"

D'mitri half-turned, snarling, "Shut up!" and Jason saw his opening. He took a step back and launched a kick as hard as he could, connecting with D'mitri's knee. D'mitri cried out and crumbled.

"Run!" Jason yelled, and he and Gary made a break for it.

"You better run!" D'mitri yelled, struggling to his feet.

The Industrial District was sixteen square blocks of empty streets and abandoned buildings. After years of playing hide and seek, kick the can, and plain old-fashioned tag, the boys could navigate its back alleys and loading docks blindfolded. They cut right at the first intersection and ran two blocks before Gary slowed to a stop.

"What are you doing?" Jason said. "They're coming."

Gary put his hands on his knees.

"Why'd you do that?" he asked.

"I'm not letting him take my computer."

"You can just build another one. Now they're going to kill us."

"They're not going to kill us."

"They're totally going to kill us."

"We're just two little kids. Why would—"

The buzzing sound of an engine firing up stopped him mid-sentence. A moment later, D'mitri and his friend squealed around the corner of the intersection on their motorcycles.

D'mitri pointed a club at them.

"You're dead!" he yelled.

"See?" Gary said.

The boys did the only thing they could do. They ran. Gary first, Jason close behind. It was no use. The motorcycles were too fast. They gained on the boys no matter how hard they pushed. D'mitri spun the club in his hand, toying with them. He sped closer and closer, ten feet, five feet, two feet, cocking his arm, ready to strike. He rode right up beside Jason and swung it at his head. Jason ducked and stumbled, falling to the side and knocking Gary into an alley. It was a dead end, but in front of them lay an open manhole. Jason ran for it, but Gary held back.

"Jason, no."

Jason, already halfway in, said, "You want to wait for them?"

"What about the sniders? And the sceels?"

"Single Corp got rid of them, remember?"

"Yeah, but—"

The motorcycles buzzed closer again, and Gary threw a panicked glance over his shoulder.

"Wait for me!"

The sewers had been built over a century before. They were wide and dark, and the water, though only ankle-deep, was cold. The boys huddled next to the ladder, shivering. Their breathing echoed through the tunnel.

"H-how long should we wait?" Gary asked.

"Until they leave," Jason said.

"How long is that going to be?"

As if to answer, D'mitri yelled down to them from the open manhole.

"YOU LITTLE JERKS ARE LUCKY I DON'T WANT TO GET MY BOOTS WET!" he yelled. "SEE YOU AROUND!"

There was a scraping sound, then what little light that filtered in through the hole disappeared. D'mitri had blocked them in.

"What are we going to do?" Gary said.

Jason took his laptop out of his backpack and opened it up. The glow of the monitor illuminated the tunnel around them. Before them, the tube receded into the darkness. It was the only direction they could go.

"I guess we go that way," he said.

So they did.

The water grew deeper and deeper. It reached their knees. Their waists. Pretty soon it was up to their chests. Jason had to hold his laptop over his head.

"Are you sure we're heading in the right direction?" Gary asked.

"There's only one."

"The water's freezing. I can't feel my toes."

"Don't be such a ba—"

Gary shrieked.

"Something just rubbed my leg!"

"That was my leg, dummy."

"No! On the other side!"

"It was probably just a log or something."

"Gross."

"Not that kind of log."

"Jason, I want to go back. I don't care if I have to wait all night. Those guys won't be up there forever."

"They blocked the opening, remember?"

"Yeah, but—"

"Shh!"

"What? Is it them? Did they find us?"

"Shut up!" Jason hissed.

Gradually they both heard it. A rushing sound. The current grew stronger, then a wave rushed down the tunnel and they were swept forward. Gary pulled away, moving faster and faster.

"Help!" he yelled, and shot around a bend.

Jason went under, still holding his computer over his head. He resurfaced, gasping for air, the sound of the rushing water growing louder and louder. All of the sudden he was weightless, flying out over a waterfall in the dark. He slammed into something and hit hard ground.

The surface he landed on was cold and rough, like concrete. He reached out behind him and felt a solid wall that seemed to be made up of sticks, dirt, and leaves.

"Gary?"

"Over here."

His voice was weak, as if he was just waking up.

"Are you okay?"

"No. I hit my head."

Jason had to find his laptop. Without its light, he was blind. Would it work even if he did find it? He slapped around, and his hand landed on something soft and squishy. He drew it back with a hiss.

"What are you doing?" Gary asked.

"Looking for my computer."

"Your computer?"

"We need the light."

"I don't feel so good, Jason."

"I know. Let me find my computer and we'll get out of here."

He slapped down on something metal and his heart leaped, but it was too narrow to be his computer. It was . . . it was a sword. A strangely shaped sword, fat in the middle before coming to a point. He pulled it to his side, just in case he needed it. Then his hand hit something square and metal and—

"Yes!"

He felt for the edge of the clamshell case and opened it, saying, "Please work, please work, please work."

Nothing happened for a moment, then the screen came to life, filling the area with cold light. The glass was cracked, and a number of keys had popped off, but it worked. The OS whirred to life. He shined it around him.

They seemed to have landed on a concrete island in the middle of the sewer. On one side the water rushed over the edge of the tunnel they'd been in, streaming down into a deep, dark hole. On the other was a dam that blocked the way. It was made out of dirt and sticks and other debris: old toys, chunks of wood and furniture—whatever trash that had been washed down into the system. He got to his feet and spun around.

"Gary I—"

Gary lay face down on the edge of the concrete island a few feet away. But that's not what made Jason pause. What made him pause was the thing rising up behind his friend.

It was a huge snake. With spider's legs. He remembered it from the Tlek war. A snider. Looks like Single Corp hadn't cleaned out every tunnel after all.

Its hood unfurled, and its red, gleaming eyes blinked to life. Electricity traced the outline of its body. Sniders were one of the Single Corps' military projects: half organic, half machine, they were designed just as much to instill fear as they were to fight.

A rattle filled the air as the snider grew to its full height, and Jason had to choose. The sword or the computer. The Single Corp hybrids were connected to the mega-secure Single Corp servers, but that didn't mean they weren't hackable. Jason knew his system had already picked up its IP address. Once he had that, all he needed to do was find an open port, get inside, and shut it down. But he needed time, and it didn't look like the snider was going to give him any. So the sword it was.

It scrabbled onto the concrete island, gathering Gary to its slimy body. A compartment opened up and he shoved the boy inside.

"Gary!" Jason yelled.

That was a mistake.

The monster turned its red eyes on him. It slunk forward, legs scrabbling the air. Jason backed away. He held the laptop up, thinking he might be able to . . . what? Hack into the creature with one typing hand? But the snider's eyes followed the light of the screen, back and forth, back and forth.

"You like the light?" Jason asked.

He swayed the computer like a pendulum. The snider swayed along, hypnotized. Jason knelt, his hand searching for the sword.

"That's it. Nice snider monster. Look at the laptop."

His hand found the handle to the sword and he picked it up, the metal scraping the concrete. The snider drew back at the sound, its rattle filling the pipe. It struck, faster than Jason could imagine, aiming for the laptop. He pulled away, dropping his machine, and the snider engulfed it in its mouth. Jason saw his chance and swung the sword at one of its legs.

It chunked into a joint, sparks flying. Another compartment in its belly opened up spit something out. The snider hissed and spun around, its tail knocking the sword out of his hand. It skidded over the edge and down the hole, disappearing forever. The monster dove down after it, and then it was gone.

Jason stood there, shocked. He felt dizzy and weak, and he fell to his knees. He was alive. He couldn't believe it. He was alive! Oh my gosh.

But Gary. Poor Gary. He'd been sucked into that compartment. And . . . OH MY GOD HE JUST SURVIVED A SNIDER ATTACK!

The thing that had shot out of the snider's belly started to beep, and he got up to see what it was. He had thought maybe he'd wounded it somehow, maybe cut off one of its circuit boards, but that's not what happened. He shuffled over and saw that it was a brace. A . . . a Barrel Arm Biceps™ brace.

"Whoa," he said.

He'd seen the ads for it before, feed images of boys fighting off bullies, video of construction workers lifting full dumpsters, but he never thought he'd actually see one in person. They cost thousands of dollars. He and his mom could barely afford groceries. He picked it up, marveling at its construction, the perfectly formed joints, the lines of super-reinforced magnesium alloy. The whole thing was engineered to mimic bone, tendon, and muscle, from the shoulder to the wrist. And the glove at the end, which the ads boasted was made out of "flexi-titanium," was as hard as metal and as pliable as skin. He turned it over and was shocked to see what was embedded in the back.

"An NES controller," he whispered.

An idea suddenly struck him. He had to rescue Gary, but that thing was bigger and faster than him. Now he knew exactly how to beat it.

~

The apartment was quiet when Jason slid the dumbwaiter door aside. He sat there for a moment, listening, before stepping onto the ancient hardwood floor. He knew every dead spot and creak, but so did his mother.

"Mom?" he called.

Nothing.

Was she working? Sometimes she picked up an extra shift at the Single Corp. He left the Barrel Arm Biceps™ in the dumbwaiter and padded across the living room, ducking under the loft where he slept, trying his best to step only on the soft spots on his way to his workshop, what his mother called his "closet."

It really was a closet, but they'd removed all the shelves and transformed space where he could stand and work on his computers. It was a tight fit, but he was still small enough to make it work, at least until he got too involved in a project and let the computer components and wires spill out into the living room. He'd almost reached the door when the toilet flushed and his mother came out of the bathroom.

"Where have you been?" she demanded.

"I just went out to play baseball with Gary."

She folded her arms across her chest.

"I'd appreciate a little communication, young man."

"Sorry, mom."

She took a few steps closer.

"What is that smell? You're dripping wet! Were you playing in the sewers again?"

"What? No, I—"

"Oh my gosh, Jason. Go get in the bath. And hang your clothes up when you're done. I can't wash them until next payday, so you'll just—"

"But Mom!"

"No 'but mom's. You stink. Go."

Jason slouched away, groaning.

"And clean up your closet when you're done," she added. "I stepped on one of your board thingies and nearly sliced my toe off. I didn't bring that stuff home for you to mangle me with it."

He took the fastest shower in the history of showers. When he came out, his mom was already gone. She left him a note.

"Picked up a shift. Back tonight. CLEAN YOUR CLOSET!"

Yes. Perfect.

He put on his only other pair of jeans and an old shirt and went to his workspace. His latest project sat on the table, almost complete. A new tablet. Stronger than anything he'd built yet, comprised of the parts his mother "borrowed" from Single Corp. She never referred to what she did as stealing. She always said she 'brought it home' for him, but Deuce wasn't dumb, and neither was his mother. She might not have known just how powerful the gear was, but she knew what she was doing. He unplugged the charger and turned the tablet on. A few keystrokes later and he brought the DOS online.

"Come on," he said, typing in the commands. "I know you're out there. Where are you?"

A string of numbers cascaded down his monitor. IP addresses. Every system currently online within a ten-mile radius. The stream seemed to last forever, and Deuce bounced on his toes, waiting for it to finish. When it finally did, he simply pinged his laptop's address and held his breath. The cursor blinked on his screen. Blink blink. Blink blink.

Nothing.

"Oh come on!" he yelled.

He pinged it again, and again he found nothing.

Okay, he thought. *Third time's a charm.*

He entered the code and closed his eyes, his finger hovering over the enter key.

"Please," he said.

He hit the key.

The numbers poured down the screen.

He pinged his address.

Blink. Blink. Blink.

Bingo!

He found it!

He located an open port and entered his username and password, and within a second he was in his old computer. He was about to run a maps search when his tablet shut down. Just went blank.

"What!" he yelled. "No!"

That had never happened before. He checked the battery. Completely charged. He checked the ports, the motherboard, the casing, the connections, everything he could think to check. It was all in perfect working order.

Then the machine whirred back to life and the snider was on his screen, staring at him. Deuce gasped. His knees went weak. It bobbed back and forth, back and forth, and then it spoke, a strange combination of hissing and insectile chatter. The translation scrolled on the bottom of the screen.

"Who dares disturb?"

Deuce looked around as if the empty apartment could give him the answer.

"Uh, me? Jason?"

The snider's head bobbed, seeming to consider this. Then it spoke again Jason didn't need the translation to understand what it said.

"Jasssssssssssson."

The hair on the back of his neck stood on end.

"Yeah. Jason."

"Why do you disturb?"

"You took my computer. A-and my friend."

"What meansssss friend?"

"My friend. Gary. He, uh, you took him."

The snider's forked tongue flickered in and out of its mouth.

"Fooooood?"

"What? No! He's a boy. Like me."

"What meansssss boy?"

"Where is he!"

"Freiiiind? Gaaaaaary?"

"Yes. My friend, Gary. Is he okay?"

The snider moved away from the screen, and there was Gary, gagged and tied to a pillar with webbing. His head slumped forward while Jason watched.

"What did you do to him?" he yelled.

The snider's face took up the screen again.

"Want Gaaaaary?"

"Yes!"

"You took from me. I waaaaaaaaant."

Jason thought for a moment.

"You mean the Barrel Arm Bicep™ brace?"

"Yesssssssssssss. You give to me, I give Gaaaaary."

The screen went black for a second, and then a map of the city popped up. A red dot blinked in the middle of the industrial district. Pinging, pinging. Jason gathered up the tablet the best he could and shoved the bundle under his arm.

Fine, he thought. *I'll play your game.*

~

He followed the blinking dot all the way across town, almost using the same path he and Gary took earlier that day. Instead of crossing Trade Street, though, it took him up to the square right outside the Silver Bullet's campus. Rows of dirty people queued along a chain-link fence, waiting for their chance to apply for a job with the Single Corp. Jason's friends made fun of them, but his mother told him not to. She said that they were homeless and helpless, desperate for work.

"They'll do anything for a job, Jason," she explained. "That's not a place anybody wants to be. They get taken advantage of."

"But don't you work for the Single Corp?"

"I do, sweetie. But it's not the same thing."

"How?"

She thought for a minute before answering.

"Let's just say I get to work on the first floor. It's not too there. But those people waiting in line? They have to work on the thirteenth floor. And nobody wants to be on the thirteenth floor."

The map led him to an alley across the street from the Silver Bullet's first guard tower. It ran behind a row of old townhouses, dead-ending with a green dumpster. The manhole cover was already off.

This time the sewer tunnel was dry and wide. It led in one direction, illuminated by glowing green moss. Jason flexed his hands in the glove, feeling the power. The brace was snug but comfortable. He felt safer with it on. Stronger too. He hadn't tried it out yet, but he'd seen the ads; he knew what it could do.

After about ten minutes, the tunnel emptied out into a large, underground space. The snider's lair. Computer components were scattered about the concrete—hard drives, cooling fans, motherboards. Gary stood at the other end. He was awake, and when he saw Jason, his eyes went wide and he started yelling despite the gag.

"Gary!" Jason cried.

He ran for his friend, and right when he reached the middle of the lair, he caught something moving in his peripheral vision. The next thing he knew, he was flying through the air. He landed hard on his back and slid a few feet. He had just enough time to roll away before the snider struck, chomping down in the air where he'd just been. He stood up and it's tail lashed out, hitting him full on in the stomach, sending him flying again. He reached out with the Barrel Arm Biceps™. The brace whirred to life, tearing up chunks of concrete as he slid backward. The snider shot for him, then drew up short to bob and wave as he got to his feet.

"Jassssssson," it hissed. "You will loooooooossssssssse."

"Oh yeah?" Jason said. He made a fist in the Barrel Arm Biceps glove. "We'll see about that."

The snider reared back and shot straight for him, faster than he could have imagined. He leaped aside at the last second, and it crashed into the concrete floor. He brought his braced arm over his head. Power surged through the brace, and he brought his arm down as hard as he could, smashing the snake over the head. It buckled and shook, and several circuits sparked and crackled. Then it collapsed and lay still.

"Yeah!" Jason yelled. "Take that!"

He ran over to Gary and ripped the web off his mouth.

"Oh my gosh, you nailed it!" Gary said.

"Hold still," Jason said, tearing at the rest of the webbing.

"I thought I was a goner. What is that thing on your arm? Where'd you get it."

"Hold *still*, Gary."

Gary's eyes went wide.

"Look out!" he yelled.

Jason tried to jump but was too late. The snider hit him from behind. This time, however, he was ready. He grabbed the pillar and swung around. He hit the ground running, and the snider turned and followed. The lair was deep and vast, held up by massive concrete pilings. Jason wove between them, dodging the monster as it attacked. It tried to shoot out in front of him, but he smashed its side with his gloved hand, sending it crashing into one of the pilings. This gave him time to double back and hide in one of the nooks. The lair fell silent. Nothing but the sound of dripping water and Jason's breathing.

Then the snider spoke.

"You are weeeeeeak, Jassssssssson," it said. "I am sssssssssssstronger than you."

It was right. Jason thought the brace would demolish it, that all he had to do was hit it once or twice and it would be crushed. But that didn't happen. How was he going to win?

"I will defeeeeeeeeeat you, Jasssssssson."

Then he remembered. The code. Use the code. He looked at the NES controller on the back of the glove. Could it be that easy? He tried it out. Up up, down down, left right, left right, B A Start. Nothing happened at first, and Jason felt his stomach turn to ice. Oh no. It was broken. He was a goner for sure. That thing was going to get him. Then another surge of power shot through the brace. The glove vibrated. He flexed his hand, and a morning star with a dozen flaming chains appeared in it. Just like in *Castlevania*. He smiled. The morning star was his favorite weapon.

He stepped out from behind the piling.
"Come and get me," he said.
The snider saw the weapon and it rose to its full height, hissing. Jason didn't miss his chance. He swung the morning star at it, connecting with its midsection, it's back, it's head. Each time he hit it, a compartment spat something out. Here a sword, there a hard drive; here a bag of coins, there a bandolier filled with knives. He struck the beast over and over. It flailed, unable to return the blows. It turned and tried to slither away, but he struck its back and it bottomed out, hitting the concrete hard enough to shake the entire lair. Jason beat it down until it was little more than a coil cowering in the corner.

"Enooooughhhhhh," it hissed. "You wiiiiiiiiin."

Jason smiled. He was a little out of breath, and the brace was warm from the amount of power he'd used.

"Leeeeeaaaave me," the snider said. "Pleeeeeeeasssss."

"Okay," Jason said. "I'll leave. But you've got to promise not to hurt anybody else or kidnap anybody else ever again."

"What meanssssss 'promisssss'?"

"It means if you say you won't do it, you can never do it."

The snider didn't reply, so Jason said, "My mom works for the Single Corp. They recalled all of you. All I have to do is let her know, and they'll come out to get you."

"Nooooooooooo!"

"Then promise."

"I . . . promisssss."

"Good," Jason said.

He cut Gary loose from the pillar, and the two of them gathered up as much of the treasure as they could. Gary strapped the bandolier of knives over his shoulders, and Jason pocketed gold coins until his pants sagged. They smiled at each other when they finished.

"Thanks, Jason," Gary said.

"For what?"

"Saving me. You didn't have to. It's kind of my fault, you know, for wanting to find a game in the first place."

"Don't worry about it. Let's get out of here."

They turned to leave, heading for the sewer tunnel.

"That thing's pretty cool," Gary said, pointing at the Barrel Arm Biceps™. "Can I try it?"

"Maybe. I want to show it to someone else first."

~

D'mitri and his gang sat over the tunnel, their bikes stashed in the brush to the side. The other Black Shirts were goofing off, play fighting and calling each other names. D'mitri glowered, staring off into the distance. He couldn't shake the memory of those two brats getting away from him. Nobody made D'mitri look stupid. Nobody. He tossed the baseball he'd taken off one of them in the air and caught it. Tossed it and caught it. On the third throw, one of his friends snatched it away.

"Knock it off!" D'mitri snapped, jumping to his feet.

The rest of the gang stopped.

"Come on, D," one of them said. "You gonna let some little kids get to you like that?"

"I said shut up!"

Jason and Gary suddenly appeared from the tunnel.

"Why don't *you* shut up," Jason said.

D'mitri turned around. A snarl crept up his lips. He hopped down, followed by the rest of his gang.

"What'd you just say?"

Jason smiled. He held up his Barrel Arm Biceps™. D'mitri laughed.

"You think that's going to stop all of us?"

"No," Deuce said. He punched the Konami code into the NES controller on the glove. The flaming morning star shot out of his palm. "But this will."

JAMES NOLL

Read on for the first chapter of *The Hive*.

JAMES NOLL

BEST DOG I EVER HAD

When most people think of an alien invasion, they think of the dumb movies Hollywood pumps out every summer. Robots and spacesuits. Lasers and spaceships. What they don't think of is the thing that dropped onto our neighbor Mr. Gomez's farm and smashed his barn to smithereens, along with his horses, his pigs, his goats, and probably about a zillion rats. We didn't see it happen, Daddy and me, but we felt it. It was seven o'clock on a Wednesday morning, and I was laid up with a broken leg on the couch, dozing in and out while I watched sitcom reruns on the TV. *Hogan's Heroes. Gilligan's Island. The Love Boat.*

   The broken leg came courtesy of Ruth Grace Hogg, starting fullback for the Caroline Cavaliers' Varsity Girl's Field Hockey team. I played forward for the Spotsylvania Knights, and for good reason, too. I lived in Spotsy, for one, and I was fleet and fast and good with my stick. Unfortunately, I didn't weigh much more than a hundred pounds. Ruth Grace Hogg tipped the scales at about a buck ninety.

I had legs like a colt. She had arms like a gorilla's.

When she saw little old me cutting up her team, she knew what she was about. She ran up to me, cocked them big hairy arms of hers, and whacked my leg like it was a piñata. Two hours later I was laid up at home on the couch, two pins in my femur and forty mgs of Vicodin in my head.

"Ain't you going to do something about it, Daddy?"

Daddy was in the kitchen, sipping a cup of coffee.

"Like what?"

"I don't know. Complain to the school board. Call the president."

"I'll get on my personal line to him directly."

"It's rude to tease an invalid. Can't you talk to her parents?"

Daddy looked like someone had just asked him to solve a calculus problem with a fish.

"Why'd I want to do something like that?"

"Because I'm your daughter. And she broke my leg. On purpose."

Daddy chuckled and shook his head.

"'Manda, you know I love you, right?"

"I'm starting to question the depths of that love."

"Well I do. But let me ask you something. You do know how much Ruth Grace Hogg weighs, right?"

"Who don't? The whole county shakes when she gets out of bed in the morning."

"And you know how much you weigh, right?"

I waited a long time before I answered. "Yeah."

"I couldn't be more proud of you. You had you a job and you didn't let nothing back you down. But you did try to run down someone nearly twice your size, and you lost. So let that be a lesson to you."

"I thought you said you were proud of me?"

"I am."

"So why're you telling me to back off the next time?"

"I didn't say that."

I ever tell you Daddy could be infuriating? I sighed, took a deep breath, and said, "You mind telling me what you are telling me, then?"

"Next time," he said. "Run faster."

So anyway, the invasion.

It was late summer, and school hadn't even started yet. The August heat and humidity weighed down on everything like a wet blanket. Our house was built in 1921, as

Daddy was fond of telling just about everybody who cared to listen. To him, that was an accomplishment. To me, it meant that nearly everything was broken or breaking down. The pipes froze every winter, the windows were like sieves, and in the summer we didn't have air conditioning. Oh, Daddy did his best. He planted a couple of recycled wheezing window units in the windows, kept them alive with a healthy application of duct tape and freon, but all they did was make a racket while blowing not-really-cold air a few feet into the house.

Daddy'd just come in from loading Sparkles up into his truck, Sparkles being an old dog of his he'd gotten stuffed. It was a sad day for the old girl. The years had been unkind, and she'd started to smell. Daddy brought her to his regular taxidermist to fix the issue, but she gave him some sorry news: old Sparkles was rotting.

"Well no shit, she's rotting," Daddy said. "She's been dead fifteen years."

Apparently pointing out the obvious didn't improve Sparkles' condition. It was finally time to lay her to rest, and Daddy was going to do it Spotsy style. He got himself ahold of a remote-controlled detonator and some explosives—cherry bombs and fertilizer and the like—and stuffed her full to the brim. The plan was simple. He and his friends were going to drive Sparkles out to the country, set her up in a field, get drunk, and blow her up.

Daddy showed me the detonator as if seeing it would make me want to go.

"You sure you don't want to come?"

"No thanks."

"Alright then."

He put it in his back pocket and went over to fill his thermos up with coffee. That's when I felt this horrible pressure build in the air. It pushed down on me, like the atmosphere itself had gone feral and decided to attack. I held my hands to my ears, but the pressure kept building and building. I opened my mouth to scream but couldn't hear anything at all. Then it released and I could hear again. A sonic boom thundered in the distance, and the house shook and rattled and nearly jumped off the foundation. I thought it was an earthquake. Or maybe Ruth Grace Hogg having a fit. I almost fell off the couch. Plates and cups clattered in the cabinets, and Daddy's ham radio fell over and cracked on the floor. Then it fell quiet and still. I pulled myself into sitting position.

"What the hell was that?"

Daddy was kind of squatting down, hands out, looking like he was waiting for another blast. His overalls were covered in coffee.

"I dunno. And don't say hell."

"You say it all the time."

The phone rang and I gasped. I could tell he wanted to chew me out, but something big had just happened, and when the phone rang after something big had just happened, you answer it.

"Aw hell," he said and snatched it off its cradle. "Yeah? Yeah, Gomez, I felt it."

He covered the mouthpiece and mouthed "It's Gomez" to me like I couldn't hear. Gomer Gomez. Our next-door neighbor. (Out here a next-door neighbor could live ten miles away.) I turned my attention back to the TV. We didn't have a remote. Not that I minded. We was lucky to even get a signal at all. I struggled off the couch and hopped over to change the channels. I was looking to see if any of the local news stations were making a special broadcast. Channel 4, nothing. Channel 7, nothing. Channel 9, nothing. Daddy kept jawing away in the kitchen.

"Calm down, Gomez. I can't understand a word you're . . . Uh-huh. Your whole barn? Uh-huh. You get a look at . . . no, I wouldn't go out there. It'd be best if you didn't. I can't,

I got 'Manda here and she's got a—" Gomez screamed something and Daddy pulled the phone away from his ear with a grimace. "Gomez? You there? Damn." And he hung up the phone.

"What's wrong with Mr. Gomez?"

"Says a spaceship landed on his barn."

Daddy went over to his gun safe and started dialing in the combination.

"Spaceship?"

"Uh-huh."

"Out here?"

"Uh-huh."

"Damn."

"Dammit, 'Manda."

"He say what it looks like?"

"Uh-huh."

"You mind telling me?"

"Said it looked like a big wasp's nest."

The gun safe unlocked with a click, and he pulled it open and started grabbing boxes of ammo. Then he took out his favorite Remington .30 .06 and slung it over his shoulder and put a couple of .357's in a bag.

"You gonna kill it?"

"Gonna try."

"Can I come?"

"You're gonna stay right here, young lady."

"Why?"

"Because you're all busted up. And if there really is a spaceship out there that looks like a wasp's nest, there ain't much you'll be able to do."

"I can shoot one of them .357s."

"I know."

"Aren't you the one who always said its better to have a man on your six?"

"Yeah, I did say that."

Daddy was already putting on his jacket and hat. He was halfway out the door.

"You really think Mr. Gomez's gonna have yours?"

That made him stop. Daddy wasn't that much of a thinker. I don't mean he was dumb because he wasn't. I mean that when a decision needed to be made, he liked to make it fast. Just like that, he said, "If you can get out to the car before I leave, you can come with me."

Mr. Gomez's farm was down Brock Road a stretch, just past Todd's Tavern. Take a few turns back toward Locust Grove, a few back roads, and there it was. Fifty acres smack dab in the middle of Spotsylvania County Virginia, the northernmost southern county in the whole damn state.

Daddy turned up the long gravel drive that led to the house, sending rocks clattering in the wheel wells and dust clouding in our wake. I bounced around in the front seat like a baby in a bucket, hoping the rifle on the rack didn't accidentally go off. Or the .357's in the bag, for that matter.

"Slow down, Daddy! You wanna break my other leg?"

He didn't reply. He had a way about him when he got set on something. He called it 'Enthusiastic Designation.' I called it 'Acting Like A Jerk'. I knew better than to bring it up. He just got cranky if I did.

He ganked the wheel and skidded to the right, steering around the side of Gomez's worn out farmhouse. Gomez was the type who liked to keep all sorts of things in his yard. Old tires. Rusted out tractors. Landscape drags and farming tillers. Daddy slalomed through it all like he was an expert, tearing up the grass, finally slowing down when he made it to the pond a few hundred yards behind the house.

Mr. Gomez's barn was just off to the side. Or it used to be. Now it was scattered all over the field like it'd been blown to bits from the inside out. In its place was something that I don't even know how to begin to describe, but I'll say this: Either Mr. Gomez'd never seen a wasp's nest in his life, or he was the stupidest man on God's green earth. The thing that landed on his barn was round and greenish-brown with spikes sticking out all over the surface. Looked more like a sweet-gum ball than a wasp's nest.

Steam or smoke or something poured off the top, and there was a crack at the bottom—an opening or a door or something—with a warm, orange light pulsing from deep inside and green stuff oozing out. And boy did it stink. Hit us full on even with the windows rolled up. I couldn't think of anything worse I'd ever smelled.

Daddy, in his usual way, summed it up nicely.

"Smells like roasted goat shit."

Mr. Gomez's neighbors were already standing in the field between the barn and the house. Mr. Sokolov and his boy, Vlad, and old Mrs. Freeman, who looked as spry as ever in her work jeans and red flannel. Mr. Gomez's sons, Gomez and Gomer, Jr, were in the middle of trying to restrain their mother who kept pulling away from them. Daddy pulled up to Mr. Sokolov's truck and put it in park.

"You stay here and watch Sparkles."

"Seriously?"

He got out without another word, leaving

his door open and the keys in the ignition. I ain't one for whining, and I'm sure he was just trying to protect me, but the day I'm compared to a stuffed dog and come out equal will be the day I can fly and shoot bullets out of my nose. I wrenched the passenger side door open, hopped out, and grabbed my crutches. It was hard going, but Daddy didn't raise no bleater, and I caught him just as he tipped his hat at Mr. Sokolov.

"Hey, Skip." (Mr. Sokolov's name was Viktor). "What's going on?"

"That thing lands on Gomez barn. Gomez, he's sucked inside."

"Sucked inside?"

"Sucked inside."

Mrs. Gomez, or should I say the Widow Mrs. Gomez, seen us, pulled herself free of her sons, and came galloping over.

"Bill! Bill, please! You've got to do something! That thing has my Gomez!"

She collapsed into Daddy's arms sobbing and carrying on, and I never saw Daddy so uncomfortable. He was not a man to show his emotions. I think they embarrassed him. And if he wasn't already embarrassed enough by his own emotions, he was damn well mortified by other people's. He patted Mrs.

Gomez on the back a few times and then peeled her off and held her at arm's length.

"Okay, Mrs. Gomez. I need to you calm down and tell me what happened."

She nodded and tried to get herself together, and after a few deep breaths, she was finally able to talk.

"Gomez went about bonkers when that thing fell on our barn. After he made a couple of phone calls, he jumped in his truck and went speeding on down here, tearing up the lawn and my peonies."

Her eyes wandered back to the house.

"I told him not to go, that this was an issue for the president, but he wouldn't listen. You know how crazy he gets about the government."

"Yes, ma'am, I do."

"He wouldn't let me go with him, neither. Me or the boys. So we watched from the kitchen window. He drove his truck right up to that thing, got out with his hunting rifle, and started shooting."

"Don't look like he did much damage."

"None at all. And then as God as my witness, when he started to reload, that crack opened up, and a tentacle slithered out, wrapped him up, and dragged him in. I don't remember what happened after that. I was too busy screaming."

Daddy looked around at everyone, seeing if he could muster them up to do something, but they toed the ground and refused to meet his gaze. Mrs. Gomez worried the front of her dress, her face reddening when she realized that nobody was going to do anything.

"If you all ain't man enough to anything, I am!"

And she marched off across the field, her sons right behind her, calling out "Momma! Momma, wait!" I tell you what, Mrs. Gomez'd worked herself up into a state. She was screaming and yelling (what exactly she was saying, I couldn't tell) tearing at her hair, jamming her finger into the air. None of us moved a muscle. She was going to do what she was going to do, whether it was good for her or not.

Daddy said, "Y'all think we should call the president?"

Mrs. Freeman spat on the ground.

"I ain't too sure what Slick Willie'll be able to do about this."

The Gomez boys did their best to stop her. Gomer jumped on his momma's back and Gomez, Jr. latched onto her legs, and they all got to screaming and yelling and clapperclawing. It might've gone on like that forever, but I guess that spiky ball'd had enough because three tentacles shot out of it, wrapped around each of the surviving members of the Family Gomez, and started reeling them in. That seemed to be enough for Daddy.

"Aw hell," he said and marched right back to the truck. He grabbed the .30 .06 off the rack and the .357's out of his bag and started loading them. "Y'all bring yours?"

He needn't have asked. Mrs. Freeman already had her shotgun out, Mr. Sokolov had a .30 .30, and Vlad'd gotten himself a machete for some reason.

Daddy, Mr. Sokolov, and Mrs. Freeman positioned themselves in a line facing the thing and started shooting. Bam! Bam! Bam! Bam! Round after round. Bullets thunked into the thing's meat, but other than a little more smoke and what looked like green syrup pouring out of its side, they did about as much harm as a squirrel chewing on an elephant.

When they were done, the air smelled like goat shit and gunpowder, but it didn't do a thing to stop the tentacles. All we could do was watch as Mrs. Gomez and her boys were sucked inside with a syrupy slurp. Daddy waited a tic before he made his final assessment of their work.

"Well, crap."

And that's when the tentacles shot out again. Four this time.

The first one grabbed Mr. Sokolov and heaved him off his feet. Another one grabbed Mrs. Freeman. The third whipped out and snatched Daddy around the waist. The last one tried to get Vlad, but he sliced it off at the tip with his machete. The tentacle went wild, spraying purple gunk all over him that burned and sizzled. Vlad fell to the ground, screaming. Daddy fixed his eyes on mine.

"'Manda," he said. "Sparkles."

Oh yeah.

Sparkles the stuffed dog. Stuffed with explosives.

I don't know if any of you ever tried to run on crutches, but it ain't like pulling a string out of a cat's ass. Hurts your armpits, too. So I dropped one and hopped back to the truck, jumped in, and turned the key. The old thing cranked to life and I slammed it into gear and stepped on the gas, aiming straight for the hive.

That old hive must've known something was up because it shot three more tentacles at me as I sped toward it. One crashed through the windshield. Another hit the grill. The third missed entirely, but swung back around and grabbed the truck by the rear bumper. It yanked sideways, and I realized I didn't even need to drive no more. The only thing I had to concentrate on was getting out before it pulled me into them slimy green and yellow guts.

I forced the driver's side door open, but one of the tentacles slammed it closed again. Another swung at me through the busted windshield and I threw myself onto the bench seat. It smashed the driver's side window and wrapped around the frame, breaking off hunks of metal. Purple ooze splattered onto the dashboard and started to eat through it. I scrambled across the seat for the passenger side door and managed to get it open, and right when I was going to dive out, praying I didn't break my neck when I landed, my broken leg exploded with pain.

It was another one of them tentacles. Damn thing'd wrapped itself around my cast and got to squeezing.

If breaking my leg was the most excruciating thing I'd ever felt, squeezing it when it was already broke ran a close second. The vision in the corners of my eyes went black and I felt like I was going to vomit. The thing yanked again, and I felt something give in my knee. I was in so much agony that I couldn't even think straight. Another squeeze, another yank. I slapped around for something, anything I could use as a weapon, and happened upon a nice, long, hunk of the metal frame.

My body was halfway out the door, and I could see the opening of the hive, pulsing and squelching as we drew near. With a scream, I sat up and stabbed that tentacle with that hunk of metal. It pulled back, ripping my cast off and sending me tumbling ass over elbows out of the truck. I flipped once and landed strange, and then I was laying on my back in Gomez's field. Next thing I heard was an explosion, and a ball of fire filled the air.

One week later, both me and Daddy were sitting on the couch eating ice cream and watching *M*A*S*H* reruns. His arm was wrapped tight to his chest and he was wearing a neck brace. He didn't like it very much, and I didn't blame him. August in Virginia was hot enough in shorts and a t-shirt without adding a neck brace. I kept catching him in the middle of taking it off, saying it "cramped his style."

"Daddy, you try to take that thing off again, I'm going to sprain your other neck."

"I don't know what that means, but message received."

My new cast was even bigger and thicker than the one before, and the itching drove me nuts, and since I wasn't allowed to take a shower, and since Daddy told me that under no circumstances was he going to give me a sponge bath, I was starting to get a little ripe. He would, though, spring for ice cream.

"I personally like me some praline myself," he said, scooping a spoonful into his mouth.

"Yuck."

I took a bite of mine, trusty, dusty Neapolitan, and watched the TV. Hawkeye and Trapper John was in the middle of fixing a prank on that old stick-in-the-mud Frank Burns again.

"Well one thing's for certain," I said. "I'm glad that old stuffed dog's finally out of the house."

Daddy gave me a playful slap.

"Don't you talk about Sparkles like that. Sparkles saved the world. Best dog I ever had."

The aliens have arrived,
and they are not friendly.

THE HIVE
AND OTHER STORIES
JAMES NOLL

My name is Amanda. Amanda May Jett. My daddy and I live in Spotsylvania County, VA, where we enjoy the fresh air and a healthy farmer's lifestyle.

At least until an alien hive crashes to earth and kills our neighbors.

It's up to us to stop the invaders and save the world, no matter how many tentacles, body-snatchers, and brain-cracking fungi they send our way.

The Hive: Season 1 is available right now! Buy it on Amazon or on my website:

www.jamesnoll.net/thehive

A NOTE FROM AMANDA

Hey y'all! It's Amanda. Amanda May Jett from Spotsylvania County, Virginia. Hopefully you're doing well. Better than us, I guess.

While I got you here, do you think you could do us a teensy favor? The guy who was kind enough to write my story makes a living off these kinds of things, and it really helps if somebody who read his books left a review. Even if they didn't like it.

So if you could find a way to go to Amazon or Goodreads or wherever and leave him one, that'd be great!

ACKNOWLEDGMENTS

Thanks to all of my readers, many of whom took a risk on a guy at a table at a convention somewhere. You guys are the best!

Also, thanks to everybody on the Self-Pub Superstars group on Facebook for their kind words, help, and encouragement.

Indie Authors Unite!

ABOUT THE AUTHOR

James Noll is a freelance writer, an educator, a musician, and a novelist from Fredericksburg, VA. He's published three other books: *A Knife in the Back*, *You Will Be Safe Here*, and *Burn All The Bodies*. *The Rabbit, The Jaguar, & The Snake* is is fourth novel and the first in The Bonesaw Trilogy. *The Hive: Season 1* is the first installment of a serial series that will be completed over the course of 2018. Check out his work at www.jamesnoll.net

Made in the USA
Columbia, SC
03 March 2018